OUR TOWER

For the children past, present and
future living in Towers everywhere.
May you always be inspired by the
heights of your homes, that reveal
endless horizons.
~J.C.

For Fran
~R.J.

OUR TOWER

JOSEPH COELHO   RICHARD JOHNSON

Frances Lincoln
Children's Books

Our Tower is grey.

Concrete and grey.

Boring, hard and grey.

But Our Tower is high
so very high.
From its fabled height
we can see rushing waves of green
beyond the grey of the estate,

beyond the black of the roads,
beyond the aches of our legs.

From the window of Our Tower
we see a tree gazing up at us
with big leafy brows.

It sings in rustles and whooshes.
Rustles and whooshes
that only we hear.
That the passers by
down below
cannot hear.
Have forgotten how to hear.

But we do
and the song vibrates within us.

Down the steps we creep,
past the lifts and bin chutes
and the bags of rubbish and door mats,
away from the overheard coughs and barks.
Away from the satellite dishes.
We creep away from Our Tower.

Past the cars on the streets
and the flickering lampposts
to the fields and woods
that border our estate.

The tree that we see
from atop Our Tower
is in a wood
but which tree?
Which tree
is the tree with bushy brows
singing the song of rustles and whooshes?

The bark of the first tree
is smooth to the touch,
too smooth to be an old singer.

The bark of the second tree
is sappy and wet.
Too sad to gaze at the Tower.

But the bark of the third tree is old ...

... old and wrinkled,
warm and cracked
and from a crack a song is spilling,
a song of rustles and whooshes.

The crack widens
and the song sucks
and the trunk is deep
and we tumble in.

At the bottom of the tree
is a world that is secret that Our Tower never sees.
That the lifts have never groaned for,
where concrete steps have never been
a world deeper than anything Our Tower has ever seen.

There are creatures lurking
between the pebbles on the ground.
There are things making ear-aching noises
that sing with a hacking coughing sound.

There are figures that flit like shadows
painted across the earthen walls.
There are thundering snarling beasts
forever chasing balls.

And when you turn into the chamber
of the mushroom glowing night
there are gleaming metallic visions that soar,
zigzag and take flight.

And on the spiky tendrils
of the most labyrinthine roots
you can taste the sweet deliciousness
of the steaming pudding fruits.

Sitting in a wooden hug
of an old and tree-grown throne
is a wizened, tree-grown man
with bushy brows and a gaze that is well known.

He saw the Towers rise
with cranes and concrete.
He saw the lifts lift
the people up from the street.

He saw us wander and creep
from Our Tower way up high
and he has ...

... a stone for us!

A stone for us!

A stone for us!

A stone so smooth and ordinary
but with a hole right through its middle
and when we peer through it
the world goes upside-a-diddle.

The things that are fantastic
in the world beneath Our Tower
now look terribly ordinary
just roots and mushrooms and flowers.

But as we rise up the trunk
that is both so high and so deep
and climb out from the tree cracks
that sing and whoosh and weep …

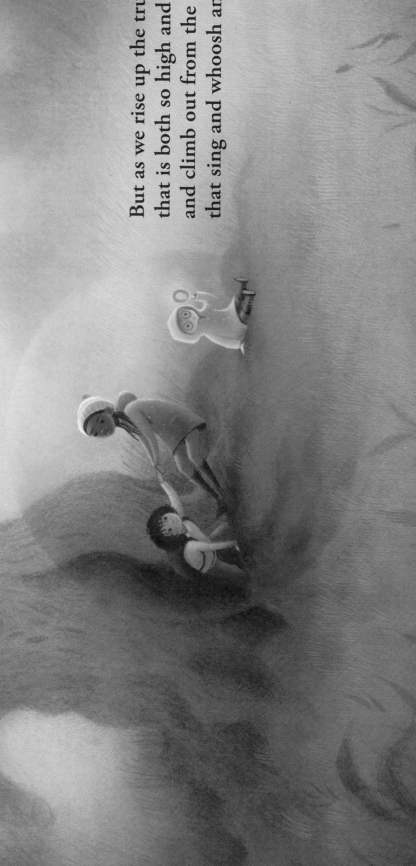

... we gaze upon Our Tower,
towering up above
and through the stone-hole
see the Tower has eyes ...

... eyes that are full of love.

We see the concrete brows
that the balconies now make.
We see the elevator mouth
that laughs as it shakes.

And as the stone guides us
to the magic of our flat
we see the wondrous creatures
that dance on each door mat.

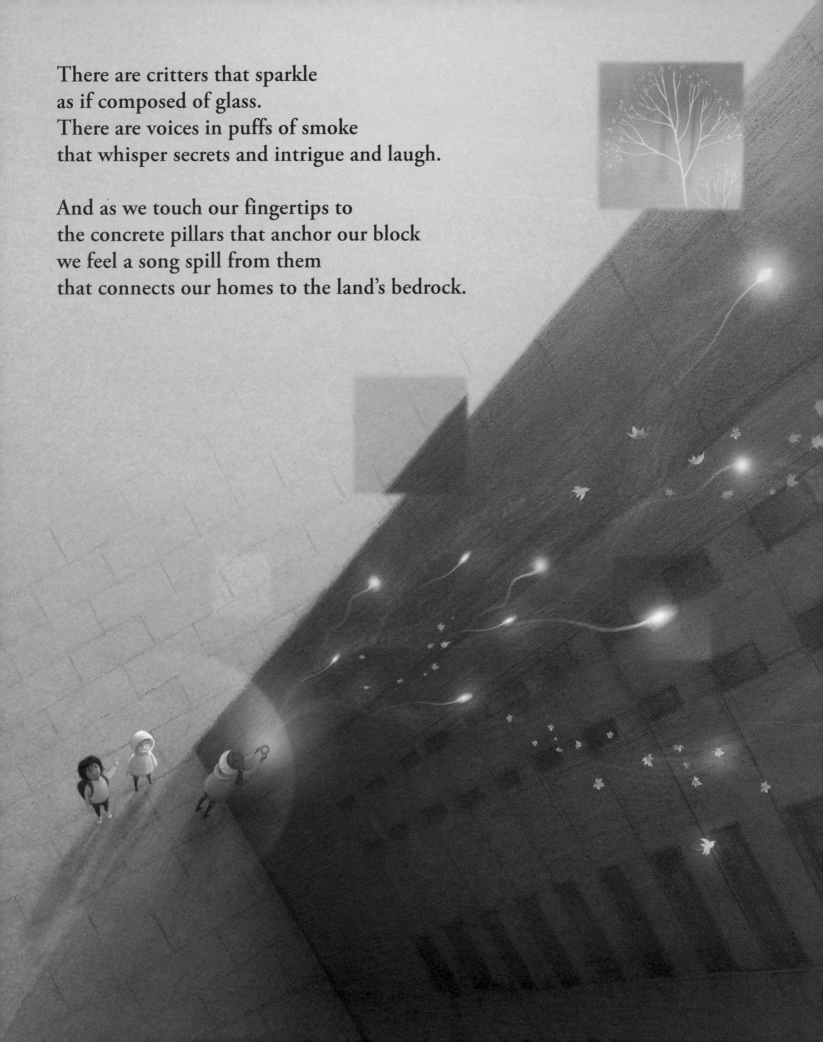

There are critters that sparkle
as if composed of glass.
There are voices in puffs of smoke
that whisper secrets and intrigue and laugh.

And as we touch our fingertips to
the concrete pillars that anchor our block
we feel a song spill from them
that connects our homes to the land's bedrock.

And the adults don't remember
the wonder of Our Tower
or that a hole in a stone can reveal how
the humdrum can hide a flower.

The adults knew, but then forgot
the wonder of the tree-grown throne
but you'll remind them of the secret
of a power that is home-grown.

A power that resides
in the smiles of our neighbours.
A magic that seeps out
when we swap our home-baked flavours.

An enchantment that sparkles
from the holding open of the lift-door.
A gratitude that radiates
when two carry shopping to a front door.

A power that is ours
that lives deep within our bones.
A power that connects us all
to an ancient tree-grown throne.

And then we'll all see
the beauty of Our Tower
and together we'll all remember
our own, deep hidden power.